SNOWMEN
AT CHRISTMAS

Caralyn Buehner

pictures by Mark Buehner

SCHOLASTIC INC.
New York   Toronto   London   Auckland   Sydney
Mexico City   New Delhi   Hong Kong   Buenos Aires

One Christmas Eve I made a snowman,
Very fat and jolly.
I dressed him up in red and green
And trimmed his hat with holly.

I saw his arms were trembling
As if he couldn't wait;
It made me start to wonder—
How do snowmen celebrate?

I think that while I'm snug in bed
Dreaming of Christmas treats,
The merry snowmen slip away
And hurry through the streets.

They glide down snowy avenues
With lamp lights all aglow;
The sleeping city blanketed
In freshly fallen snow.

They pass by toy shop windows
Framed with twinkling lights,
Pausing for a peek or two
At holiday delights.

The jolly snowmen gather
From everywhere around,
For a Christmas party
In the center of the town.

Waving to each other
They call out cheery greetings,
All their friends and family
So happy to be meeting.

A few merry snowmen
Start trimming the square.
Soon holly and icicles
Are strung everywhere.

And then, reaching high,
For everyone to see,
They hang balls of snow
On the big Christmas tree.

The snow children play
Freeze tag or Red Rover,
Or climb in a stack
'Til they wobble right over.

The mothers lay out
All kinds of cold treats:
Ice cream and snow cones
And dainty iced sweets.

Then the dancing begins
To the tune of a fiddle,
All the snowmen line up,
And sashay down the middle.

Someone says "Hush!"
Could that be a jingle?
Then over the hill glides
The snowman Kris Kringle!

He opens his sack
With a jolly "Ho ho!"
And pulls out their presents,
Each made out of snow.

Santa sips his cocoa,
The reindeer romp and play.
And then, with a whistle,
They're off on their way.

Such fun snowmen have!
But there's still one more thing—
With hearts full of joy
They hold hands and they sing.

While the fiddler plays,
And sweet silver bells ring,
They sing songs about snow,
And the birth of a King.

The children are sleepy,
The grown-ups are yawning,
The snowmen go home
Just as Christmas is dawning.

They're all back in their places
When Christmas Day starts,
But these folks made of snow
Have a glow in their hearts.

Their smiles are more tender,
Their eyes softly shine,
As the snowmen dream dreams
Of *their* Christmastime.

MERRY CHRISTMAS!

To JaDene Denniston and all our friends at Sunrise Elementary

Readers, see if you can find a cat, a rabbit, a Santa face, a Tyrannosaurus Rex, and a little brown mouse hidden in each painting.